Mr Krispett
BOOKS
BRIMMING
WITH
IMAGINATION!

This Book Belongs To

_____

_____

_____

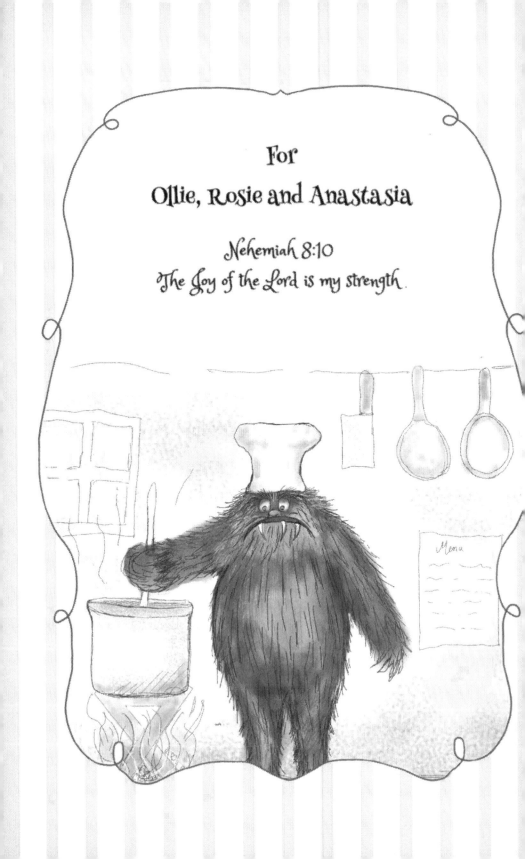

For

Ollie, Rosie and Anastasia

Nehemiah 8:10
The Joy of the Lord is my strength.

Mr Krispett's Kids Joke Book

Hundreds of Jokes and silly Poems!

Written and illustrated By Mr Krispell

First Edition

Animal Fun!

While searching for the Emu
My sister got lost at the zoo
She got into a rage
And was put in a cage
I visit when I've nout to do

How do you know
if a snake has sent you
a valentines card?
It's sealed with
a hiss.

To My darling
Mary Viper
London Zoo
cage 8

Hissssss

How do you save
a drowning mouse?
Give it Mouse-to-Mouse
resuscitation!

What's the best way
to brush your hare?
Hold its long ears firmly,
whilst brushing gently.

Why shouldn't you
listen to a farmer, when
he's milking his cows?
He talks Udder Nonsense!

What do Cats
call mice?
Delicious!

What's smelly and
jumps all over Australia?
A Kanga-Poo!

Why did the Poodle
marry the Golden Retriever?
She found him very fetching.

Where do dogs park
their cars?
In the Barking Lot!

Why couldn't Noah
catch many fish?
He only had two worms!

Where do young
cows go to lunch?
The Calf-eteria.

Where can you find
old cow bones?
In the Moo-seum

Where do sheep go
after high school?
Ewe-niversity!

What did the farmer do
when his pig had a heart
attack?
He called the
Ham-bulance!

Hambulance

What goes trot-dash-trot-dash-dash-dash?
Horse code.

What do you call
a big cat who lives by
a pond?
A Duck-filled-fatty-puss.

First cat: Where do
fleas go in winter?
Second cat: Search me.

What is Elsa the
elephant's middle name?
The.

What has large antlers,
Has a very high voice
and wears white gloves?
Mickey Moose.

What instrument squeaks
when you blow into it?
A Mouse organ.

What pet makes the
loudest noise?
A Trumpet!

Sign in shop window:
For Sale, pedigree Doberman.
House trained. Eats anything.
Very fond of children!

What's worse than raining cats and dogs? Hailing taxi cabs!

What dog won't stop crying? A Chi-Wa-Wa.

Where do frogs keep their jackets? In the Croak room.

Where do ants go to eat, after a hard days work? To a Restaur-ant.

How do cats keep their soda cold? Mice cubes.

What fish do you meet in hospital? Sturgeons!

How do you communicate with a deaf pig? Use Swine language!

What's as big as a Hippo yet weighs zero pounds?
A Hippo's shadow.

How did the farmer know that the fox stole his chicken?
The pig squealed on him.

How do you stop an elephant from smelling?
Tie a knot in his trunk.

What do you give a sick pig?
Oinkment.

Oinkment

What was the tortoise doing on the highway?
About ten yards an hour.

What do you give a sick lemon?
Lemonade.

What's grey has four legs and a trunk?
A mouse going on vacation.

What do you call someone who cuts the sea bed?
A prawn-mower

How do cats celebrate when they move into a new home?
With a Mouse-warming party.

"Excuse me, do you have any dogs going cheap?"
"No sir, ours just go Woof Woof."

What do you get if you cross a sheepdog with a bunch of tulips?
Collie-flowers.

What do you call a pony with a cough?
A little horse!

What bird sits in a field with binoculars?
A Stare-crow.

How does a chicken tell the time?
One O' Cluck, two O' Cluck, Three O' Cluck

What kind of language
do hedgehogs speak?
Spine language.

What type of shoes
do bears wear?
None, they go bear foot.

What do you get
if you cross a dog with
an omelet?
Pooched eggs.

Why do cows lie
down in the cold?
To keep each
udder warm.

What did the mouse
say when he broke
his teeth?
Hard cheese!

What do you get if
you pour hot water down
a rabbit hole?
Hot cross bunnies!

How do chickens communicate with each other?
By Walkie-turkey!

Knock, Knock

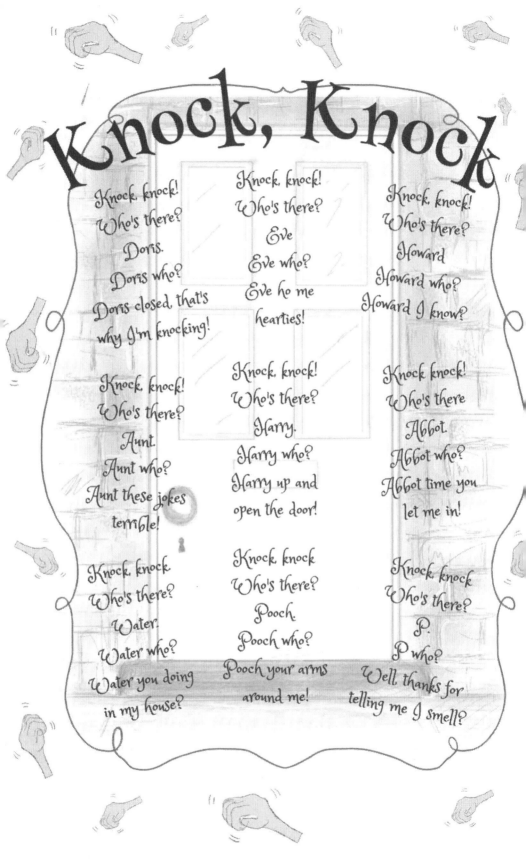

Knock, knock!
Who's there?
Doris.
Doris who?
Doris closed, that's
why I'm knocking!

Knock, knock!
Who's there?
Aunt.
Aunt who?
Aunt these jokes
terrible!

Knock, knock
Who's there?
Water.
Water who?
Water you doing
in my house?

Knock, knock!
Who's there?
Eve
Eve who?
Eve ho me
hearties!

Knock, knock!
Who's there?
Harry.
Harry who?
Harry up and
open the door!

Knock knock
Who's there?
Pooch.
Pooch who?
Pooch your arms
around me!

Knock, knock!
Who's there?
Howard
Howard who?
Howard I know?

Knock knock!
Who's there
Abbot.
Abbot who?
Abbot time you
let me in!

Knock, knock
Who's there?
P.
P who?
Well, thanks for
telling me I smell?

Knock, Knock

Knock, knock
who's there?
Boo.
Boo who?
Don't cry it's
only a joke.

Knock, knock
who's there?
Howard.
Howard who?
Howard I know.

Knock, knock
who's there?
Water.
Water who?
Water you doing
in my house?

Knock, knock
who's there?
P.
P who?
Well thanks for
telling me I smell.

Knock, knock
who's there?
Yah.
Yah who?
Are you a cowboy
or something?

Knock, knock
Who's there?
Cook.
Cook who?
Have you been
eating bird food?

Knock, knock
who's there?
Ammonia.
Ammonia who?
Ammonia little girl
let me in!

Knock, knock
who's there?
Aunt.
Aunt who?
Aunt you going
to let me in?

Knock, knock
who's there?
Pooch.
Pooch who?
Pooch your arms
around me.

Knock, Knock

Knock, knock
Who's there?
Ketchup.
Ketchup who?
Ketchup with me
and I'll tell you

Knock, knock
Who's there?
Eve.
Eve who?
Eve Ho my
hearties!

Knock, knock
Who's there?
Olive.
Olive who?
Olive next door.

Knock, knock
Who's there?
Athena.
Athena who?
Athena monkey in
your garden.

Knock, knock
Who's there?
Tish.
Tish who?
Bless you, here's
a hankie.

Knock, knock
Who's there?
Barbara.
Barbara who?
Barbara black sheep
have you any wool?

Knock, knock
Who's there?
Lee King.
Lee King who?
Lee King bucket.

Knock, knock
Who's there?
Irish stew.
Irish stew who?
Irish stew in the
name of the law!

Knock, knock
Who's there?
Ewan.
Ewan who?
Nobody else, just
me.

Candy Dream

If the world was made of candy
If the world was made of cake
I'd cross the sherbet desert
To reach the chocolate lake
I'd spend the whole day swimming
With toffee crocodiles
Not one of them is angry
They wear marshmallow smiles
At sunset I'd go skiing
On the Mountain of Sorbet
Then ride a cotton candy cloud
To Treacle Custard Bay
A vanilla fondant pillow
Is wear I'd lay my head
And the sweetest dreams I'd dream
In my cookie crumble bed

Why was the small cookie crying? Because it's mum had been a wafer so long.

Why were the crowd booing at the cookie boxing match? They were watching crummy fighters!

Who sits in a bowl and moans about the custard being too hot? Apple Grumble.

Who sits on a cake and sings? Icing Sugar.

Did you hear about the jelly and sponge who had a punch up? They were put into custardy. How did they feel after? A trifle worried.

A triffle worried

Johnny: what does your dad put on his rhubarb? Jack: Manure. Johnny: Yuck. I prefer custard.

What do you get when two strawberries meet? A Strawberry shake!

Boy: Did you like the chocolates Mrs Smith?
Mrs Smith: Yes, very much.
Boy: That's funny. My mum said you didn't have any taste.

What is white and yellow, and throws itself off the edge of the dinner table? Lemming Meringue!

What cake wanted to rule the world? Attila the Bun.

Did you hear about the cornflake? Don't worry I'll tell you next week, it's a cereal.

What do you call a rabbit dressed up as a cake? A cream bun.

How do you grow
a big crop of liquorice?
Plant lots of Ani-seed!

Why was the gingerbread
house in a state of disrepair?
It had been desserted
years ago.

Why was there a lot
of noise in the kitchen?
Because the banana split,
so the ice Screamed!

What do you call a
sheep coated in chocolate?
A chocolate baaaa!

How do you lock
the door of a
gingerbread house?
With Coo-keys!

How many idiots does
it take to make chocolate
chip cookies?
Six— One to make the
dough and five to peel
the M&M's.

How do you start
a Jelly race?
On your marks, Get Set, go!

CHOCOLATE Baa!
MADE IN RAMSGATE

How do elf's make
sandwiches?
With shortbread.

Did you hear about
the chocolate factory?
It melted.

Elf
Shortbread
Made with Elf-raising flour

What's the best thing
to put into a chocolate
cake?
Your teeth!

Chocolate
Factory

What candy do fish
prefer?
Bubble gum.

What cake gives you
an upset stomach?
Rocky road.

How do you make
a cream puff?
Chase it around the
garden.

How did Hansel and
Gretel keep their
teeth clean?
With Candy Floss!

Doctor, Doctor

Doctor, doctor
Everyone keeps
thinking I'm a liar.
I don't believe you.

Doctor, doctor
I need something
to keep my falling
hair in.
Here's a bag.

Doctor, doctor
I keep thinking
I'm an electric eel.
That's shocking!

Doctor, doctor
I can't get to
sleep.
Don't worry, sit
on the edge of
your bed, you'll
soon drop off.

Doctor, doctor
I'm having trouble
breathing.
I'll give you something
that will soon put a
stop to that.

Doctor, doctor
I have amnesia.
Take these pills
and you'll soon
forget about it.

Doctor, doctor
I keep thinking
I'm a needle.
I don't see
your point.

Doctor, doctor
I keep thinking
I'm a bridge.
What's come over
you?
A large truck, two
cars and a coach.

Doctor, doctor
What did the
X-ray of my head
show?
Absolutely nothing.

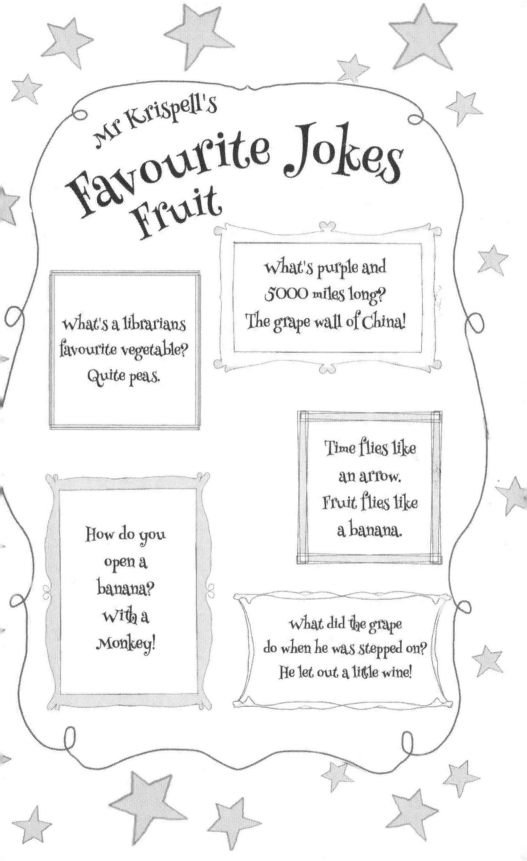

Mr Krispell's
Favourite Jokes
Fruit

What's a librarians
favourite vegetable?
Quite peas.

What's purple and
5000 miles long?
The grape wall of China!

Time flies like
an arrow.
Fruit flies like
a banana.

How do you
open a
banana?
With a
Monkey!

What did the grape
do when he was stepped on?
He let out a little wine!

Waiter Waiter

Waiter, I think I've just
swallowed a fish bone.
Are you choking?
No, I'm serious.

Waiter, there's a twig
in my meal.
Don't worry, I'll get
the branch manager.

Waiter, why is there
a fish on my plate
of spaghetti?
I'm sorry sir, it
doesn't know it's plaice.

Waiter, what's this?
It's bean soup sir.
I don't care what
it's been, what is it
now?

Waiter, there's a dead fly
swimming in my soup.
Don't be silly, dead
flys can't swim.

Waiter, there's an ant
in my soup.
I know... The flies
stay away during
the winter.

Waiter, this bread
is stale.
It wasn't last week
sir.

Waiter, there's a snail
in my salad.
Don't worry, it won't
eat much.

Doctor, Doctor

Doctor, doctor
My wife smells
like a fish.
Poor sole.

Doctor, doctor
I'm a burglar.
Have you taken
anything for it?

Doctor, doctor
I've lost my
memory.
When did it
happen?
When did what
happen?

Doctor, doctor
I keep thinking
I'm a cowboy.
How long has
this been going
on?
About a Yeeehaaah!

Doctor, doctor
I feel like a dog.
Sit!

Doctor, doctor
I keep seeing an
insect everywhere.
Don't worry—it's just
a bug that's going
round.

Doctor, doctor
My baby is the
image of me.
Not to worry, as
long as he's healthy.

Doctor, doctor
I keep thinking
I'm a caterpillar.
Don't worry, you'll
soon change.

Doctor, doctor
I keep seeing
double.
Sit on the couch.
Which one?

Doctor, Doctor

Doctor, doctor
I feel like a
pack of cards.
I'll deal with
you later.

Doctor, doctor
I keep thinking
I'm a moth.
So why did you
come here then?
Well I saw this
light at the widow.

Doctor, doctor
I get pains in one
eye when I drink
coffee.
Have you tried
taking the spoon out.

Doctor, doctor
People keep on
ignoring me.
Next!

Doctor, doctor
I keep thinking
there are two
of me.
One at a time
please.

Doctor, doctor
Will this ointment
clear up my spots?
I never make
rash promises.

Doctor, doctor
I think I'm a
snail.
Don't worry
we'll soon get you
out of your shell.

Doctor, doctor
My son has just
swallowed a roll
of film.
Let's hope nothing
develops.

Doctor, doctor
I keep thinking
I'm a yo-yo.
Not to worry life's
full of ups and downs.

Weather Fun!

A boy that wasn't that bright
Made his trousers from an old kite
He was ok until
He walked up a hill
Then his trousers blew off and took flight

Why was the lightning naughty? He didn't know how to conduct himself.

What do you call a lovely warm sunny day following two rainy days? Monday!

He gets the weekend off →

Why wouldn't the cloud talk to the hurricane? They had a stormy relationship.

What do you call a women with a storm on her head? Gail.

What animal never gets wet? An Umbrellaphant

What's very clever and fills the sky with Color? A Brainbow!

Who fell down a rabbit whole and got drenched? Alice in Thunderland!

What holds the moon up in the sky? Moonbeams!

What do you get if you freeze a Witch? A Cold spell.

Now she's doing Witchdraft →

What do you call a Snowman on a warm day? Puddle.

How do sheep keep warm in winter? They turn on the Central Bleating.

Why shouldn't you ice skate on a full stomach? Because it's easier to skate on an Ice Rink!

What did one raindrop say to the other? Two's company, three's a Cloud.

How do you wrap
a cloud?
With a rainbow.

What do you call
it when it rains,
Chickens and Ducks?
Fowl Weather!

What do you call
a Roman Emperor
with a cold?
Julius Sneezer!

When does it rain
money?
When there's a Change
in the weather.

When do monkeys
fall from the sky?
During Ape-ril showers!

What did the tree
say after a long winter?
What a Re-leaf.

Can February March?
No, but April May!

Who invented the first
rain jacket?
Anna Rack!

What's the difference
between a lion with
toothache and a wet day?
One Roars with pain;
the other Pours with rain.

Did you hear about
the idiot who broke his
leg while sweeping leaves?
He fell out of the tree!

Why don't owls date
when it's raining?
Because it's Too wet too woo!

↑ Do not use
in trees.

Where does a Snowman
put his candles?
On his Birthday Flake!

Where did the Snowman
meet his wife?
On the Winternet!

What kind of bow
can't be untied?
A Rainbow.

Pirate Poetry

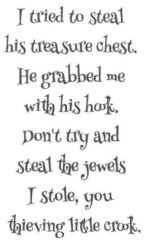

Because I wouldn't
marry him
He made me walk
the plank.
I'll love you till
the day you die
He pushed and
then I sank.

I tried to steal
his treasure chest.
He grabbed me
with his hook.
Don't try and
steal the jewels
I stole, you
thieving little crook.

I'd like to be a pirate
Robbing ships and drinking rum
My dad could be the lookout
The cook can be my mum
My sister she can scrub the decks
My cat can man the masts
If we spot a ship of teachers
My cannons they will blast

Why did Captain Hook cross the road?
To get to the second hand shop.

What does a dyslexic pirate say?
Rrrraaaaaa!

How did the pirate get his Jolly Roger so cheaply?
He bought it on sail.

What do you get if you cross Santa Claus with a pirate?
A Yo ho ho.

Why don't pirates shower before they walk the plank?
Because they'll just wash up on the shore later.

What has 7 legs, 7 eyes, and 7 arms?
7 pirates.

Why are pirates called pirates?
Because they aaarrrr!

How much did the pirate pay for his peg and hook? An arm and a leg.

What's orange and sounds like a parrot? A carrot.

What was the name of Blackbeards wife? Peg.

Why didn't anybody want to play cards with the pirate? Because he was standing on the deck.

How do Pirates prefer to communicate? Aye to aye!

How do you make a pirate furious? Take away his p. irate.

Have you heard any good pirate jokes? Well neither have ayyye!

Mr Krispell's
Favourite Long Jokes!

Mum: Come on Jack, get dressed; you'll be late for school.

Jack: I don't want to go to school. The teachers don't like me, the children don't like me—even the caretaker doesn't like me!

Mum: You're just being silly.

Jack: Why should I?

Mum: Well, for one thing you're forty three years old, and for another you're the headmaster!

Mum: Why are you crying?

Son: Dad hit his thumb with a hammer.

Mum: Knowing you, I'm surprised you didn't laugh.

Son: That's the problem—I did!

Hee Hee! Ho ho! Hee Hee! Ha ha! Ha ha! Ho ho! Hee Hee! Ho ho! Hee Hee! Ho ho! Ha ha! Ha ha! Hee Hee! Ho ho! Hee Hee!

What do you call?

What do you call a man with a seagull on his head?

Cliff.

What do you call a man with a rabbit up his jumper?

Warren.

What do you call a girl with a frog on her head?

Lilly.

What do you call a nun with a washing machine on her head?

Sister Matic.

Waiter Waiter

Waiter, please be careful
your thumb is in my soup.
Not to worry sir, it isn't
very hot.

Waiter! What's this footprint
doing on my pie?
Waiter: Well you did ask
me to step on it, sir.

Waiter, these potatoes taste
funny.
Then why aren't you laughing
sir?

Waiter, this egg is bad.
Don't blame me sir, I only
laid the table.

Waiter! Get me the manager,
this food is disgusting.
Waiter: He won't eat it
either, sir.

Menu

Waiter, do you serve fish?
Of course sir, we'll serve anyone.

Waiter, bring me something
to eat and make it snappy!
Crocodile sandwich on its
way, sir.

Waiter, will my pizza be long?
No sir, it'll be round of course.

Waiter Waiter

Waiter, I've just found a
slug in my lettuce!
Don't worry sir we
not charge you extra.

Waiter, what's that fly doing
in my soup?
Appears to be the
backstroke, sir.

Waiter, my plates all wet.
That's your soup, madam.

Waiter, is there lasagna
on the menu?
Yes, I'll get a cloth
And wipe it off.

How did you find your
steak, sir?
Well I just moved a
chip and it was there.

Waiter, do you have
frogs legs?
No it's just the way
I walk.

Waiter, what's this fly
doing on my ice cream?
Looks like its learning
to ski sir.

Waiter, there's a wasp
in my soup.
I think you'll find its
a vitamin B.

Waiter Waiter

Waiter, I think I've just
swallowed a fish bone.
Are you choking?
No, I'm serious.

Waiter, there's a twig
in my meal.
Don't worry, I'll get
the branch manager.

Waiter, why is there
a fish on my plate
of spaghetti?
I'm sorry sir, it
doesn't know it's plaice.

Waiter, what's this?
It's bean soup sir.
I don't care what
it's been, what is it
now?

Waiter, there's a dead fly
swimming in my soup.
Don't be silly, dead
flys can't swim.

Waiter, there's an ant
in my soup.
I know... The flies
stay away during
the winter.

Waiter, this bread
is stale.
It wasn't last week
sir.

Waiter, there's a snail
in my salad.
Don't worry, it won't
eat much.

Crazy Fun!

I once knew a girl called Hannah
Who used to eat food with a spanner
Every time that she ate
She'd smash every plate
In the most peculiar manner

What do you get if you cross a cow with a volcano?
Udder disaster.

Why wouldn't the bogeyman go out on Friday night?
Because he was all dressed up with nowhere to goo.

He wants to go out and boogie

Why was the duck sent to the headmasters office?
He kept on making wisequaks.

What do you call a bird that laughs at everyone?
A mockingbird.

Why did the nose hate going to school?
Because he was tired of being picked on.

STOP KIDS PICKING our NOSES

Why was the archaeologist crying?
He hit rock bottom because his career was in ruins.

Who invented a plane that wouldn't fly? The Wrong brothers.

Where does Tarzan get his clothes from? A jungle sale!

Jungle Sale

What insects can tell the time? Clockroaches!

tick tock

What do you call a mad young octopus? A crazy mixed up squid!

KEEP OUT OF MY TANK

How do you cut an ocean in half? With a sea-saw.

What's small white and smells? A pong pong ball.

Pongy! have you been playing stable tennis?

What grows on a wall? A Walnut!

Bang! Bang! Bang! Bang! Bang! Bang! Bang! Bang! Bang! Bang! Bang! Bang!

Where do butchers dance?
At a meatball.

"We'll meat again"

Why did the stamp
need a lawyer?
It was ripped off.

"Don't address me like that!"

Why did the fishmonger
go deaf?
He lost his herring.

Why did the elephant
leave the circus?
He was tired of working
for peanuts.

Did you hear that
the fire-eater got
engaged?
He ran into an
old flame.

"I've got a hot date tonight."

Where do spies shop?
At the snoopermarket.

Beans

Why did the baker
stop making donuts?
He was tired of the
hole thing.

"I don't knead the dough anymore."

Christmas Fun!

Silly sailor Sally
sailed the seven seas
Her sails were sown of silken threads
Her masts of Christmas trees

What did one snowman say to the other.
Do you smell carrots?

What did Adam say the day before Christmas?
It's Christmas Eve.

What's green covered in tinsel and eats flies?
Mistle-toad.

Did you hear about the thief who stole a Christmas calendar?
He got 12 months.

What goes: Now you see me, now you don't, now you see me, now you see me?
A snowman on a Zebra crossing.

How does
Good King Wenceslas
like his pizza?
Deep and crisp and even.

What do you get
if you eat Christmas
decorations?
Tinsell-itis!

The first sign of Tinselitis

Who did Father
Christmas marry?
Mary Christmas.

Son: Can I have a budgie
for Christmas?
Mum: No, you can have turkey
like the rest of us.

What do guests sing at
a snowman's birthday
party?
Freeze a Jolly Good Fellow.

Why does Father Christmas
come down the chimney?
Because it soots him.

Funny Clothes

I once knew a girl called Eileen

Who lived in a washing machine

She dined with a frock

Then married a sock

And never again was seen

What coat feels wet when you put it on? A coat of paint!

Sister: This dress fits me like a bandage.
Brother: Did you buy it by accident?

Bought by accident

Gentleman: Can I try those trousers on in the window?
Snooty shop assistant: We'd prefer you tried them on in the changing room, sir!

Where can you buy a cheap elephant? At a Jumbo sale.

Jumbo Sale

I stand corrected. said the man in orthopaedic shoes.

Lady: Do you sell crocodile shoes?
Assistant: what size feet does your crocodile have, madam?

Who's the boss of the hankies?
The Hankie-chief.

Why did the opera singer have such a high voice?
She had falsetto teeth.

La La

What does the Queen do if she burps?
Issues a royal pardon.

To whom do people always take off their hats?
Hairdressers.

Tom: My dad went swimming and all his clothes were stolen.
Jim: So what did he come home in?
Tom: The dark.

Coat of Arms

What coat has many sleeves?
A coat of arms

In which tree should you hang your underwear?
In a pantry— or a vestry!

Sally: Every time I'm down in the dumps, I get myself a new outfit.
Tom: I was wondering where you got them from.

The dumps

What do you call a butchers assistant?
A chop assistant.

Sausages on sale
5 for the price of 6

Did you hear about the man who put a new pair of shoes on every day?
By the end of the week, he couldn't put his shoes on

Did you hear about the two silk worms that had a race?
It ended in a tie!

Sally: For my birthday, I'd like a dress that matches my eyes.
Tom: Where can you buy a bloodshot dress?

What do you get if you pull your underwear up to your neck?
A chest of drawers!

School Fun

I like my teacher very much
She is funny and she's kind
When my dog ate my homework
She didn't seem to mind
The next day with my Homework
She handed me a bone.
And then she gently smiled at me
Clever, funny, Mrs Sloan

Teacher: How did the Vikings communicate with each other?
Pupil: With Norse Code!

Teacher: You have half an hour to write an essay on Hadrian's wall.
Pupil: But miss I'd rather write on paper.

It was built a long time ago!!

Son: Dad I think my teacher really likes me.
Dad: Whys that son?
She keeps putting kisses on my homework.

Teacher: If I had seven apples in one hand and ten oranges in my other hand what would I have?
Pupil: Very large hands!

Dad: How was your first day at school son.
Son: My new teacher doesn't know anything, all he does is ask questions!

Teacher: What word do you always spell incorrectly?
Pupil: Incorrectly!

Why did the Elf
fail his exams?
He didn't do his
Gnome work

Which Queen suffered
indigestion?
Queen Hic-toria.

Why did Henry the VIII
have so many wife's?
He liked to chop and change.

Teacher: You, boy, name me
two pronouns!
Boy: Who, me?
Teacher: Correct!

Teacher: Where were traitors
beheaded?
Pupil: Just above their
shoulders!

Teacher: Does any one
know anything about
Ancient Greece?
Pupil: They serve it in
the canteen miss!

Ancient grease found
in school canteen

Teacher: What does minimum
mean?
Pupil: A very small mother!

Minimum   **Maximum**

Teacher: Paul, did your sister help you with your homework?
Paul: No, miss, she did it all

Teacher: Peter why are you late for school?
Peter: Well Sir, I was walking to school when I saw a sign that said Slow, school ahead.

 Warning slow down or you'll end up in class.

Teacher: If I cut a banana into five pieces and a apple into seven pieces what have I got?
Pupil: Fruit Salad.

Teacher: Do you know what adding is?
Paul: Yes, miss, that's the noise my door bell makes!

Teacher: Simon can you spell Your name backwards?
Simon: No, miss.

Teacher: This essay on 'My Dog' is exactly the same as your sister's!
Harry: Well it's the same dog.

If there are eight cats in a boat and one jumps out, how many are left? None, they are all Copycats!

When was Queen Victoria buried? Just after she died.

What came after the Stone Age? The Saus-age.

The saus-age began on a Fryday.

What exam must you pass before you can work in a soda drink factory? Fizzical education.

Where are the Kings and Queens of England crowned? On the head.

Why were the teachers eyes crossed? She couldn't control her pupils.

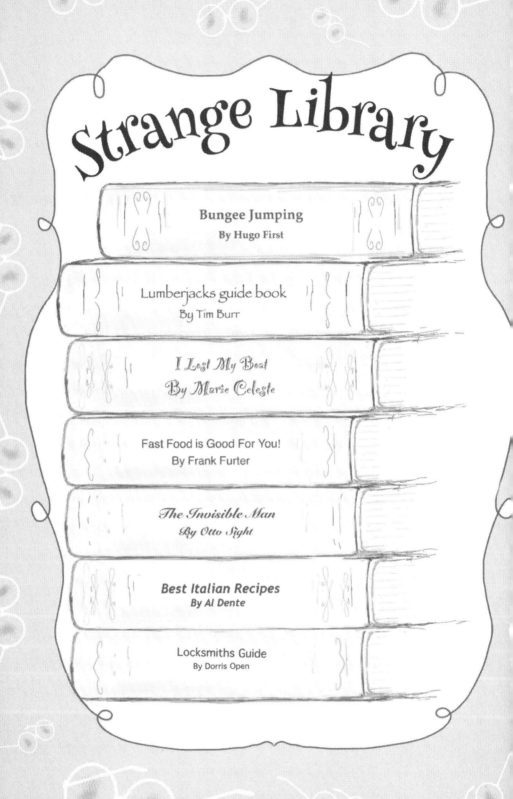

Strange Library

Bungee Jumping
By Hugo First

Lumberjacks guide book
By Tim Burr

I Lost My Boat
By Marie Celeste

Fast Food is Good For You!
By Frank Furter

The Invisible Man
By Otto Sight

Best Italian Recipes
By Al Dente

Locksmiths Guide
By Dorris Open

Strange Library

How to get a knighthood
By Neil Down

Coffee is Bad for You!
By T. Pott

Did Pirates Talk Backwards?
By Rodger Jolly

D I Y Bird Table
By Jack Daw

How to have a
White Christmas!
By Dan Druff

Catching Crooks
By Hans Upp

Make Your Own Robot
By Anne Droid

Space Poems

A Martian came to Earth
last night
I think I've got the proof
my bedrooms full of greenish slime
and now we've got no roof

I'm going to build a rocket
I'm going to the moon
I've a suitcase full of sandwiches
For I won't be back till June

I'll send school dinners straight to Mars
they'll see what Earthlings eat
We'll see their ships bypass the earth
I guess we'll never meet

What was the first
animal in space?
The cow, it jumped over
the moon.

What was the first fruit
in space?
A coco–naut

Why won't the diners
tip at the restaurant on
the moon?
It's got no atmosphere.

Where can you buy
dairy products in space?
The Milky Way.

How does an astronaut
say sorry?
He Apollo–gises.

Where do astronauts kiss
at Christmas?
Underneath the missile–toe.

How. Do you have
a successful space party?
You planet. (plan it.)

What do you call
a hot sausage in space?
An unidentified frying
object.

How do you get a
baby astronaut to sleep?
You rock-et.

What did the alien
who landed in a
garden say?
Take me to your weeder!

Why wasn't the astronaut
hungry?
He'd just had a
big launch.

Where do astronauts leave
their spaceships?
At parking meteors.

How does the solar system
keep its trousers up?
Whith an asteroid belt.

Why did the spaceship
land outside the bedroom?
Someone had left the
landing light on.

What do passing shooting stars say to each other?
Pleased to meteor!

Which is heavier: a full moon or half a moon?
A half moon because a full moon is lighter.

Full Moon

What did Mercury say to Saturn?
Give me a ring sometime.

What did Superman's parents ask him when he got home?
Where on earth have you been?

Why are aliens great gardeners?
Because they have green fingers.

Why did the atom cross the road?
Because it was time to split.

When can't you book a room on the moon?
When it's full.

Brother vs Sister

Sister: I always speak my mind.
Brother: I'm surprised you have so much to say then.

Brother: How long can someone live without a brain?
Sister: How old are you?

Brother: Mum, there's a salesman at the door with a funny face.
Sister: Tell him you've already got one!

Sister: None of these matches in this box work!
Brother: That's funny they were all working when I tested them yesterday!

Knock Knock

Knock, knock
Who's there?
Cows go.
Cows go who?
No, cows go moooo!

Knock, knock
Who's there?
Woo.
Woo hoo?
Don't get excited its
just a joke.

Knock, knock
Who's there?
Egbert.
Egbert who?
Egbert no bacon.

Knock, knock
Who's there?
Aardvark.
Aardvark who?
Aardvark a million
miles for one
of your smiles.

Knock, knock
Who's there?
Annie.
Annie who?
Annie thing you
can do, I can do
better.

Knock, knock
Who's there?
Kanga.
Kanga who?
No, it's kangaRoo!

Knock, knock
Who's there?
Pecan.
Pecan who?
Pecan someone your
own size.

Knock, knock
Who's there?
Ray.
Ray who?
Ray-member me?

Knock, knock
Who's there?
Phyllis.
Phyllis who?
Phyllis up a
glass of cola.

Insect Poetry

Bees give you honey
Bugs give you bites
Worms give you tummy aches
And spiders give you frights

To hide your bugs and insects
You need a secret place
Like your mothers slippers
Or your sisters pillow case

A spider was the head chef
The baker was a snail
They opened up a cake shop
Not one cake did they sell
But our cakes are the finest
They're made with worm and flea
Our loaves are so delicate
Spiced with wasp and bee
Why they never sold one single cake
Remains a mystery

What crazy bug
lives on the moon?
A lunar-tick.

What do you call
two spiders on their
honeymoon?
Newlywebs.

What do you call
a snail that lives on
a boat?
A Snailor.

What insects can't sing?
Humbugs.

Why did the fly fly?
Because the spider spied'er.

Why wouldn't the butterfly
go to the dance?
Because it was a moth-ball

How does a firefly
race start?
Ready steady glow!

Glow!

What's worse than finding
a worm in your apple?
Finding half a worm
in your apple.

How many legs does
an ant have?
Two the same as
an uncle.

2 the same
← as an uncle

What do you get
if you cross a parrot
with a centipede?
A walkie-talkie.

What are the slowest
creatures on Mars?
Snail-ions.

If Martians live on
Mars and Venusians
live on Venus, what lives
on Pluto?
Fleas.

What do you call
a greenfly with no
legs, arms or wings?
A bogey.

Where would you find
Giant snails.
On the need of Giants'
fingers!

I couldn't
find a frog.

Mum: Bill why did you
put a spider in your
sister's bed?
Bill: I couldn't find
a frog.

What's invisible and jumps up and down in a field all day?
A glass-hopper

You can't see it because it's invisible.

What's the last thing That goes through a wasps mind when it hits the windscreen?
It's sting.

"Ouch take him to Waspital."

How do you know which end of a worm is its head?
Tickle it and see which end smiles.

This side was tickled.

What's the difference between school dinners and worms?
School dinners come on a plate.

Why don't baby birds smile?
We'll would you smile if your mum fed you worms all day?

YUCK!

How do you keep flies out of the school canteen?
Let them taste the food

Slug: Who's that sitting on your back?
Snail: That's Michelle.

Veg Poem

I won't eat turnips
I won't eat peas
I don't like brussels
They make me sneeze
I don't like cabbage or curly Kale
I've heard it makes boys grow a tale
I don't want courgettes
I can't Stand leek
It makes your knees and elbows creak
Carrots onions parsnips foul
They'll turn a smile into a scowl
I don't want spinach or aubergines
I don't want veg or any greens
No broad beans or cauliflower cheese

Triple ice cream and jelly please!

What's slim green and goes boing-boing-boing? A spring onion.

Boing!

What do hedgehogs have for dinner? Prickled onions.

Why did the farmer drive a steam roller over his field? He wanted to grow mashed potatoes.

What did the courgette who married an onion say? "I'll love you till the day you fry!"

Why should you never tell a secret in a greengrocer's? Because the potatoes have eyes and the beanstalk.

What purple King ruled over England? Alfred the Grape!

Why did the mushroom get invited to lots of parties? Because he was a fun guy.

What did the lemon say to the orange? Anything you can do I can do bitter.

What's yellow and always points north? A magnetic banana.

How do you make a peach punch? Give it boxing lessons.

What fruit teases you a lot? A ba..na..na..na.

What sits in a fruit bowl and cries for help? A damson in distress.

What do you call an oversized pumpkin? A plumpkin.

Why was the peanut crying? He'd just been asalted.

"That hurt my peelings!"

"Ba-na-na-na-na"

Dinosaur Fun!

At the bottom of my garden
There was a dinosaur asleep
I tickled him under arm
He didn't make a peep
I whistled him ten merry tunes
He didn't even stir
Then I sat a cat upon his ear
He couldn't hear him purr
A mountain of petals
I placed beneath his nose
Pebbles, sticks, and apple cores
I crammed between his toes
Finally from the shed roof
I jumped onto his nose
Then miracle of miracles
The dinosaur arose
He didn't seem that friendly
There was an angry roar
So I refused to play with him
That rude dinosaur!

Where did the T. Rex live?
Anywhere it wanted.

What do you call a dinosaur that eats gunpowder?
A Dino-mite.

What do you call fossilised bacon?
Jurassic Pork.

Why did the T. Rex wear plasters?
He had Dino-sores.

How do you cut a Triceratops in half?
With a Dino-saw.

DINO SAW

How do you brush a Sabre toothed tiger's teeth?
Very carefully.

What bird used to work in a bakery before becoming extinct?
The dough dough bird.

Where can you buy
a T. rex from?
A dino-store.

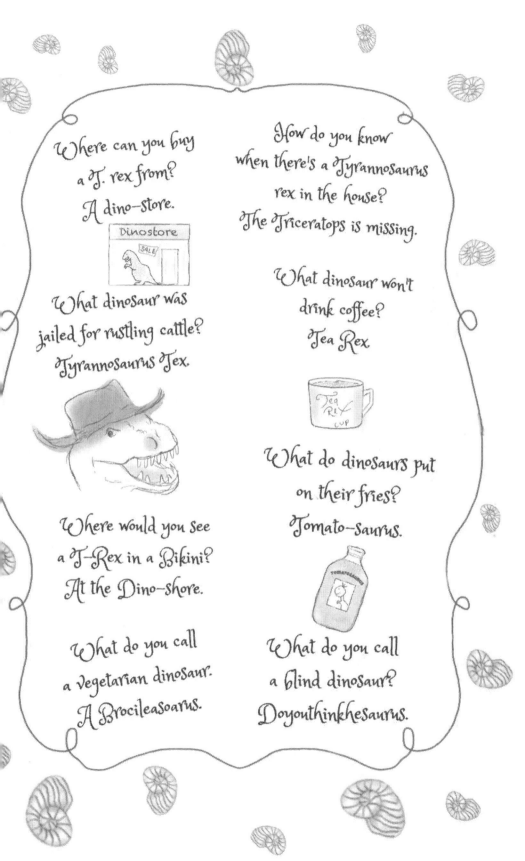

What dinosaur was
jailed for rustling cattle?
Tyrannosaurus Tex.

Where would you see
a T-Rex in a Bikini?
At the Dino-shore.

What do you call
a vegetarian dinosaur.
A Brocileasoarus.

How do you know
when there's a Tyrannosaurus
rex in the house?
The Triceratops is missing.

What dinosaur won't
drink coffee?
Tea Rex

What do dinosaurs put
on their fries?
Tomato-saurus.

What do you call
a blind dinosaur?
Doyouthinkhesaurus.

Monster Fun

I dined with a monster I knew
so proud of his big pot of goo
Carrots and bats
Ferrets and rats
I spent the next week on the loo

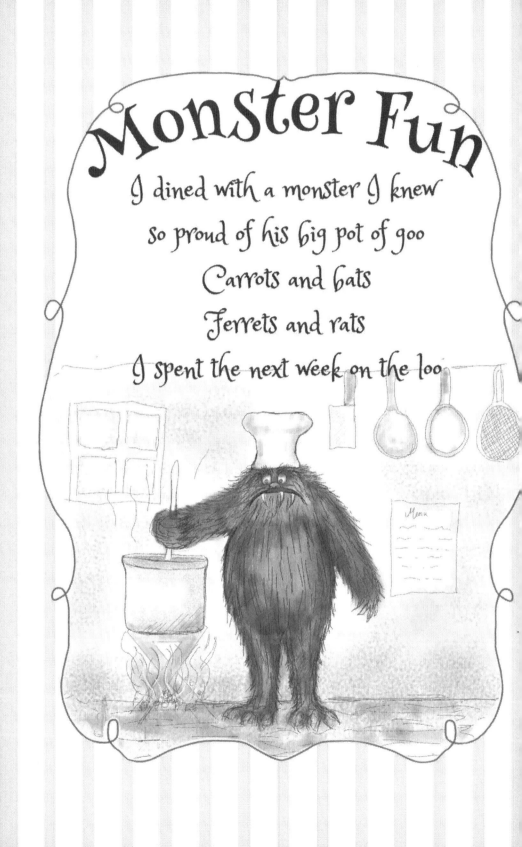

What's it like to be kissed by a vampire? A pain in the neck.

OUCH!

What do you do with a green monster? Wait until he ripens.

Why didn't the two four-eyed monsters marry? They couldn't see eye to eye.

Why were all the monsters booing in the theatre? They were watching the Abominable Showman.

Where do you store werewolfs? In a Were-house.

WEREHOUSE

Why don't monsters eat clowns? Because they taste funny!

YUCK!

What do you call a nervous witch? A twitch.

BOO!

GET OFF!

What's a werewolf's favourite day of the week? Moonday.

Why are graveyards so popular? Because everybody's dying to get in.

What time does Dracula visit the dentist? Tooth hurty!

02:30

Who did Frankenstein take on a date? His Goul-friend.

What can you find between Godzilla's toes? Slow runners!

Why was there no food left at the halloween party? Because everyone was a goblin

What's the largest building in Transylvania? The Vampire State Building.

Who do you call if you've a spooky bread bin? Toastbusters!

TOASTBUSTERS

What monster hides in your handkerchief? The bogey monster.

Don't worry he's snot that scary!

How do you know when there's a monster under your bed? Your nose touches the ceiling.

What's the best way to talk to a monster? On the phone.

Hi Monster. How ya doing?

1234 5678 90

Why should never upset a cannibal? You might get into hot water.

What do you call a monster that devours everything in his path? Lonely.

Royal Fun

I once knew a Queen who was barmy

She wore a dress of salami

But by the end of the week

The whole palace did reek

And she was marched to the bath

By her army

Pupil: I wished I'd lived in the olden days.
Teacher: Why?
Pupil: There wouldn't be so much history to learn.

History is so easy!

When was King Arthur's army too tired?
When they'd had too many sleepless Knights.

DO NOT DISTURB
zZZZ

Which Queen of England had the largest crown?
The one with the largest head.

What's the difference between the death rates of the Middle Ages and today?
There isn't, it's still one death per person.

What did one knife say to the other?
Look sharp.

A Swiss army knife

Why are soldiers so tired on April 1st?
They've just completed a 31 day March.

What did the executioner say to his wife?
Only 30 chopping days before Christmas.

Who invented King Arthur's round table?
Sir Cumference.

Inventor →

What does the Queen do after she burps?
Issues a royal pardon.

Why did the Queen draw straight lines?
Because she's a ruler.

Why did the Queen go to the dentist?
To get her teeth crowned.

A STRAIGHT TALKING QUEEN

During which battle was Lord Nelson killed?
His last one.

Where did King Charles keep his armies?
Up his sleevies.

Who invented fractions?
Henry the Eighth.

Mr Krispell's
Favourite Long Jokes!

Hairdresser: How would you like it, Madam?
Lady: Could you cut it very short on one side and not at all on the other, with a short stubby fringe at the front, and big tufts pulled out at the back?
Hairdresser: Oh dear, I don't think I can manage that, madam.
Lady: Why not? You did last time.

One day, two big tortoises and a little tortoise went into a café. They ordered three strawberry milkshakes. While they were waiting it began to rain.
'Oh dear,' said one of the big tortoises. 'We should have brought our umbrella.' 'Yes' said the other big tortoise. 'Let's send the little one back to get it.'
'I'll go,' said the little tortoise, 'but promise me you won't drink my strawberry milkshake while I'm away.'
Well, the two big tortoises promised not to touch his strawberry milkshake, and the little tortoise set off.
A few days later one the big tortoises said 'let's eat his strawberry milkshake anyway.' At that moment the little tortoise shouted from the back of the café, 'You do that and I won't fetch the umbrella!'

Music Fun

Why was the musician arrested?
He got into treble.

Why are pianos grand?
Because they're so upright!

Did you hear about the boy who played recorder in tune?
Neither did I.

What's a cats favourite musical?
The sound of mew-sic.

Piano tuner: I've come to tune your piano.
Pianist: But I didn't call you.
Piano tuner: No but your neighbours did.

What do you call a piano with only white keys?
A minor problem!

What vegetable has great rhythm?
Beat-root.

Sea Fun

I joined the sea scouts of Kent

But we camped under sea in a tent

"It's no use complaining,

at least it's not raining"

Said the scout leader of Kent

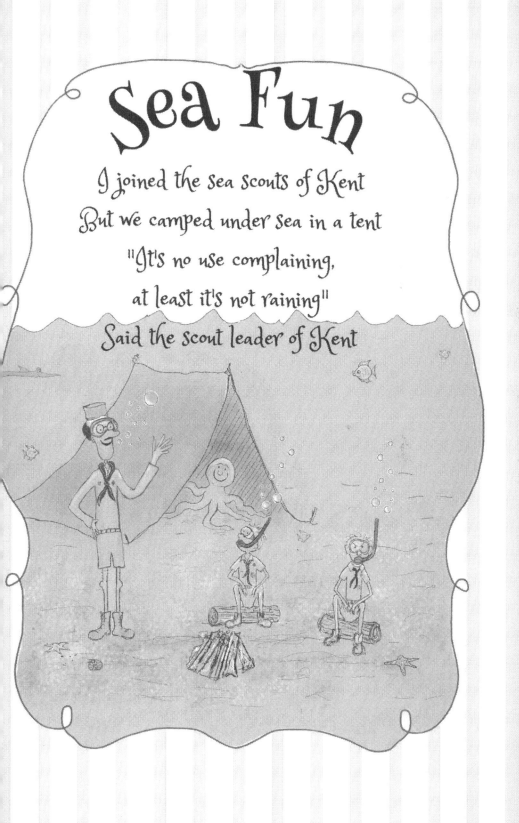

What kind of hair does the ocean have?
Wavy.

What's got one large hand, one small hand and sharp teeth?
A Clock-adile!

Why do fish like worms?
Because they're hooked on them!

What day do fish hate most?
Fryday!

What did the fish call his date?
His Gill-friend.

What did the boat call her date?
Her buoy-friend.

Who stole the baby octopus?
A Squidnapper.

What lies at the bottom of the sea shivering? A nervous wreck.

What do you call a frog with no hind legs? Un-hoppy.

Where does a sick ship go? To the dock.

ALL SEA SICK SHIPS REPORT TO DOCK!

What kind of cats love water? Octopuses!

Doctor, doctor I smell like a fish! Oh you poor sole!

Where would you weigh a whale? At a Whale Weigh Station!

Did you hear about the cargo ship carrying potatoes, that run aground in a storm? It caused a giant Chip wreck!

What do you call a man with a seagull on his head? Cliff!

What do you call a girl with a bucket and spade on her head? Sandy!

What do you call a man floating in the sea? Bob!

Why was the mermaid so bitter? She grew up with a ship on her shoulder!

What did the small sardine say when it saw a submarine? Look mum a tin of people!

Tinned People Yummy!

Why did the bird sit on the fish? The fish was Perch!

Why does it take pirates so long to learn the Alphabet? They spend years at C.

Why does the ocean Roar? Well, wouldn't you if you had crabs on your bottom!

Mum: How are your marks at school Bill?
Bill: They're underwater.
Mum: What?
Bill: They're below C.

How far can a pirate ship go? 20 miles to the Galleon.

Why was the lobster sent to jail? He kept on Pinching things!

How much do Pirates pay for their earrings? A Buccaneer!

€1 →

What do you get if you cross a river with a sea? Wet!

Who's in jail at the bottom of the sea? Billy the Squid! What was his crime? He robbed a river bank!

Looney Fun

Snotty nosed Sarah
Sneezed a snotty sneeze
She sneezed bogeys on the flowers
She sneezed bogeys on the trees
If you want to find her garden
It's easy to be seen
For in every single season
Her garden is still Green

What do you call
a sheep that's going mad?
Baaa-rmy!

Two ducks are on a motorbike.
The one on the back says, 'Quack'
and the other one says, I'm
going as quack as I can.

Quak!
Quak!

Dinner: My fish isn't cooked.
Waiter: How do you know?
Dinner: It's eaten all my chips

Who's safe when a
man eating tiger is
on the loose?
Women and children.

What's for
dessert?

What did the policeman
eat for lunch?
Truncheon meat.

He should of
had toast.

Did you hear about
the man who drowned in
a bowl of muesli?
He was pulled under
by a strong currant!

What goes to bed
with its shoes on?
A horse.

A man goes into a
pet shop and says, 'I'd
like to buy a wasp please!.'
'Sorry sir. We don't sell
wasps.' 'Well you've got one
in the window.'

Which is the laziest
mountain in the world?
Everest.

Taxi driver: Please can
you tell me if my indicators
are working?
Passenger: Yes, no, yes, no, yes
no, yes, no,

What are brown and
sneak around the kitchen?
Minced spies!

What do you call
a failed lion tamer?
Claude Bottom.

What happens if you fall asleep under a car? You wake up oily in the morning!

Why did the germ cross the microscope? To get to the other slide.

What do you do when the forth bridge collapses? Build a fifth bridge.

What lives in a pod and is a Kung-fu expert? Bruce Pea.

These photographs you've taken don't do me justice. You don't want justice you want mercy.

What do you call a blind reindeer? No eye deer.

Cat Fun

If Kittens
        we're mittens
They'd make the
        the purr-fect gift

If lions
    we're irons
All creases soon
        would shift

If Tigers
        we're taxis
You wouldn't want
            a lift

What do you call a women with a cat on her head?
Kitty.

What's a cats favourite TV programme?
Mews at ten

What do you get if you cross a cat with a lemon?
A sourpuss.

← A very bitter cat

1st cat: What have you done for your fleas?
2nd cat: Nothing, why should I? They've never done anything for me.

Jim: I'm looking for a one eyed cat called Tibbles.
Jack: What's the other eye called?

Jim: What's the difference between A cats litter tray and a pizza?
Jack: I don't know.
Jim: I'm not coming to dinner at your house then!

Bill: We had to have
our cat put down.
Jack: Was she mad?
Bill: Well, she wasn't
too pleased.

Bill: Our cat's just
like one of the family.
Jack: Really? Which one?

Jack: Have you ever
seen a fox trot?
Bill: No, but I've seen
a cat nap. zzZ
ZZZ

Bill: In the park I
was surrounded by lions.
Jack: Lions in the park?
Bill: Yes, dandelions

Why shouldn't you
stand on a cat's tail?
It hurts it's felines.

What cat should you
never play cards with?
A cheetah.

Mum: Did you put the
cat out?
Bill: Was it on fire
again?

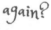

Elephant Fun!

Excuse me My Elephant
I wonder if you know
You're feet are rather heavy
And ones upon my toe.
I'm from a land called England
We don't like to make a scene
But if you do not move it

I will have to SCREAMMM!

I saw an elephant down the street
I said why do you hide In custard
He looked at me like I was mad
"Well... It's too hot to hide in mustard"

Why is an elephant
so wrinkled?
Have you ever tried to
fit one on an ironing
board?

What do an elephant
and a strawberry have
in common?
They're both red except
for the elephant.

What happened after Ray
was stepped on by an
elephant?
He became an X-ray.

Why didn't the elephant
enjoy his holiday?
The airline lost his trunk.

How do you get down
from an elephant?
You don't, you get down
from a duck.

Why did the elephant
paint his feet yellow?
So he could hide upside
down in custard.

Did you hear about the elephant that had a nervous breakdown? They had to give him trunquilizers!

What goes up slowly and down quickly? An Elephant in an elevator.

What do you call an elephant in a phone booth? Stuck.

What did the elephant say when he walked into the grocery store? Ouch!

Grocery Store

OUCH!

What's large, gray and hard to spot? A stain resistant elephant.

Waiter! What's this elephant doing in my alphabet soup? Waiter: I guess he's learning to read.

Elementary English

Trunquilizers

Trunquilizers

Love Fun!

I once knew a Prince too small
Who loved a Princess too tall
He grew sadder and sadder
Until he found a ladder
And took it along to the ball

What do you sing when two cookies get married? Here crumbs the bride.

Boy: I told my girlfriend that she was drawing her eyebrows to high.
Friend: Then what happened? She looked surprised.

Girlfriend: Whisper something soft and sweet in my ear.
Boyfriend: Lemon meringue pie.

Boy: Do you have a date for Valentine's Day.
Girl: Yes, February 14th

What did one boat say to the other? Are you up for a little row—mance.

Knock, knock
Who's there?
Olive.
Olive who?
Olive you and I don't care who knows it.

Did you hear about the two turnips that got engaged? They became Swedehearts.

Train Announcement

The train now arriving on platforms 3, 4, and 5 is coming in sideways!

How can you tell
If a train has just
passed you?
You can see it's tracks.

Why are railroad
tracks angry?
Because people are
always crossing them.

What do you call
a train that eats toffee?
A chew, chew train.

Miss Stuffy: Porter, how long will
the next train to Inverness be?
Porter: About 150 metres madam.

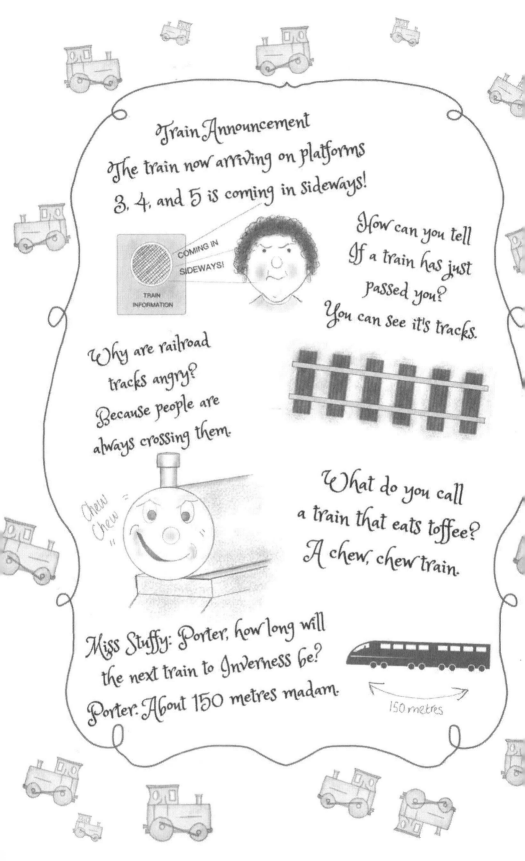

What do you give a
sick lemon?
Lemonade.

Orange
Squash

Lemonade

I've lost my memory.
When did you lose it?
When did I lose what?

? ? ?

Who's at the door?
A man with a drum kit.
Tell him to beat it.

What do you give a
sick bird?
Tweetment.

What did the first
mind reader say to
the second mind reader?
You're alright how am I?

How am
I?

How do I do?

If two's company and
three's a crowd, what's
four and five?
Nine.

How did the Cowboy count his livestock?
With a Cow-culator.

2+8

What do Cowboys put on their salad?
Ranch Dressing

Why did the Indian ride his horse?
It was to heavy to carry.

Did you hear about the two cowboy bakers?
They had a Bun fight at the O.k. Corral.

I can make you speak like a red indian.
How?
See I told you I could.

How!

Why did the Cowboys car break down?
It had Injun trouble.
(engine trouble)

Where do you send
an injured bee?
To a Waspital.

What does a Snail
do on his birthday?
He Shellebrates!

"Happy Birthday
to you, your brains
full of goo!"

How do you find where
a flea has bitten you?
Start from scratch.

What do bees chew?
Bumble Gum.

Bumble Gum

How do bees get
to school?
On the school buzz

How does a Nit get
from place to place?
By Itch-hiking!

Where did Noah keep
his bees on his Ark?
In the Arc-hives.

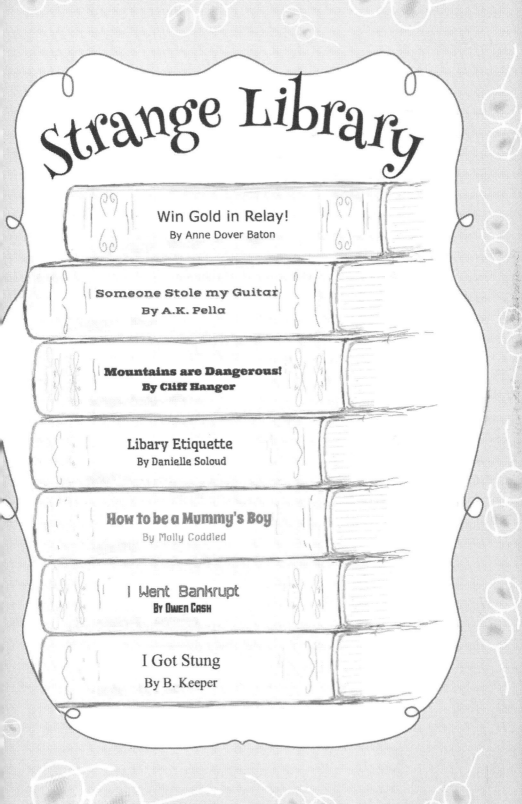

Strange Library

Win Gold in Relay!
By Anne Dover Baton

Someone Stole my Guitar
By A.K. Pella

Mountains are Dangerous!
By Cliff Hanger

Libary Etiquette
By Danielle Soloud

How to be a Mummy's Boy
By Molly Coddled

I Went Bankrupt
By Owen Cash

I Got Stung
By B. Keeper

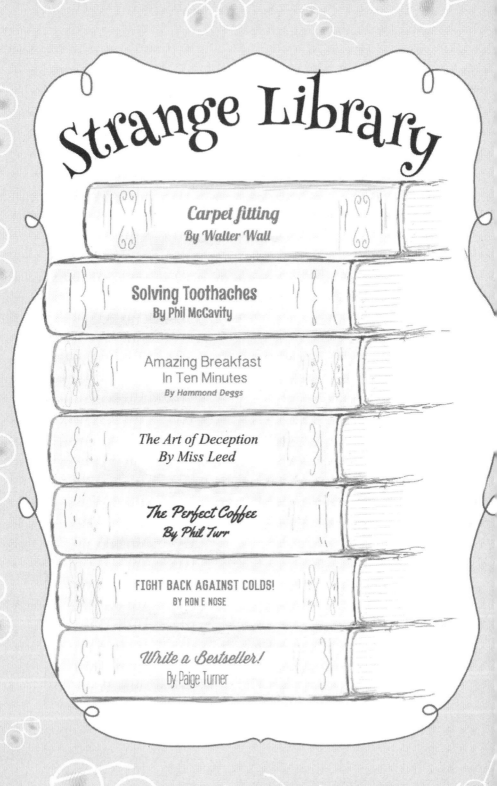

Strange Library

Carpet fitting
By Walter Wall

Solving Toothaches
By Phil McCavity

Amazing Breakfast
In Ten Minutes
By Hammond Deggs

The Art of Deception
By Miss Leed

The Perfect Coffee
By Phil Turr

FIGHT BACK AGAINST COLDS!
BY RON E NOSE

Write a Bestseller!
By Paige Turner

Mr Krispell's
Favourite Jokes

He loves them so much he even framed them.

What has two horns and
gives us milk?
A cow!
What has one horn and
gives us milk?
A milk truck!

Why didn't the wooden spoon
get married?
He wanted to be a spatular
(Bachelor)

What does a spider's
bride wear?
A webbing dress.

How can you
find space custard?
With a Jellyscope!

How does a monkey
ring the bell?
King Kong! King Kong!

Mr Krispell's Favourite Jokes

He loves them so much he even framed them.

What's green misty
and croaks?
Kernite the fog!

What's pink and
cloudy?
A pink cloud.
What's blue and
cloudy?
A pink cloud
holding its breath!

What's E.T
short for?
He has
little legs!

What's blue and
smells like
red paint?
Blue paint.

What should people
who live in glass houses do?
Put the toilet in
the cellar.

What do you call?

What do you call a man with
a number plate on his head?

Reg.

What do you call a woman with
two toilets on her head?

Lulu.

What do you call a Queen with
a heavy lopsided crown on her head?

Queen Eileen.

What do you call a camel with
no hump?
Humphrey!

What do you call?

What do you call a man with
potatoes, meat and gravy on his head?

Stew.

What do you call a man with no legs?
Neil.

What do you call a man with
leaves on his head?

Russell.

What do you call a man with a
bag of compost on his head?
Pete.

What do you call a man with a
car on his head?
Jack.

I love my uncle even though
He's very Silly!

One day he took up tap dancing.
But he fell into the sink!

He bought a lovely tie from a shop.
But took it back because it was too tight.

MY UNCLE

He bought a pair of water skis.
Then got fed up when he couldn't find a lake with a slope.

He got sacked from his job at the banana factory.
He kept on throwing all the bent bananas out!

He bought a two piece jigsaw puzzle.
He never finished it because he lost the lid!

He failed at climbing Mount Everest.
He said he ran out of scaffolding!

One day he fell out of a window and broke his leg.
He was ironing the curtains!

Tongue Twisters

They are harder than they look!
Try and do these in ten minutes.
Why not get someone to time you...

Toasted treacle tigers taste terrific

Frozen fleas weren't free to flee

Tenderly tickled teapots, tend to tumble out tea hee

Peculiar Petula from Peru parcelled pickled parrots to Timbuktu

Two witches, two watches, which witch wore what watch?

General Gerald generally generalised in January

Greedy grinning goblins grab ginormous grubs

Terribly tough tongue twisters tend to give tired tongues blisters!

Congratulations!

Very Silly Signs!

All these signs are real!

Outside a chip shop:

WE FOUND NEMO. FISH SANDWICHES ARE BACK!

Sign in men's toilet:

We aim to keep these toilets clean! Your aim will help!

Sign inside a shop:

ANYONE CAUGHT EXITING THRU THIS DOOR WILL BE ASKED TO LEAVE!

Sign outside a house:

BEWARE OF THE DOG! The cat is not trustworthy Either.

Sign in delicatessen:

Our tongue sandwiches speak for themselves!

Outside safari:

BEWARE

WILD ANIMALS/ CHILDREN

Very Silly Signs!

All these signs are real!

Sign outside office:

ATTENTION

THE FIFTH FLOOR HAS TEMPORARILY BEEN MOVED TO THE SEVENTH FLOOR!

Sign outside shop:

Come in
We're
CLOSED

Sign outside a hotel:

FREE WI-FI

STARTING AT €59 DOLLARS

Sign inside a park:

No signs Allowed!

Sign down a street:

KEEP
←
RIGHT

Sign outside flats:

Warning!

Bicycles chained to these railings will be moved without notice

THIS IS A NOTICE!

The Jokes I left out!

I didn't tell you the joke about the bed.
Because it hasn't been made yet!

I didn't mention the joke about the dustbin.
Because it's rubbish!

I left out the joke about Pinocchio's nose
Because it was too long!

I left out the joke about the blunt pencil.
Well there's no point!

I was going to tell you the joke about the old mans foot.
But it's too corny.

I decided not to mention the joke about the drill!
It's too boring!

And the funny joke about butter?
I thought you'll only spread it.

And Finally!
NEWS FLASH!

A ship carrying red paint collided today with a ship carrying brown paint. Both crews were marooned.

A robber stole a van load of soap today. Police say they tried their best to capture him but he made a clean getaway.

Today we talk to an out of work contortionist who says he can no longer make ends meet.

A cement mixer collided with a prison van on the highway today. Motorist are asked to look out for 12 hardened criminals.

A 4-foot man and a 9-foot man have just escaped from jail. The police are looking high and low for them

A Lorry load of wigs have been stolen in New York. Police are combing the area.

The End!

I hope enjoyed reading this book
as much as I did writing it!

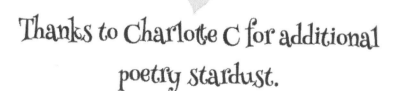

Thanks to Charlotte C for additional
poetry stardust.

Mr Krispell is also author of:

✳ ✳ ✳ ✳

Grumble Mumble Grumble

✳ ✳ ✳ ✳

The Princess Everything Book

✳ ✳ ✳ ✳

Why won't Arnold come out to play?

If you're loosing sheep go find a shepherd
If you're loosing sleep go find a good shepherd!

Mr. Krispell Books
Maida Vale, London
rakispell@gmail.com

Editor & additional poetry stardust: **Charli Wood**

Mentor & page layout: **bndn**

Printed in Great Britain
by Amazon